JALEN'S BIG CITY LIFE

MOVING DAY HELPERS

T0372084

by **Dorothy H Price** illustrated by **Shiane Salabie**

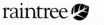

raintree

a Capstone company — publishers for children

Raintree is an imprint of Capstone Global Library Limited,
a company incorporated in England and Wales having its
registered office at 264 Banbury Road, Oxford, OX2 7DY –
Registered company number: 6695582

Edited by Alison Deering
Designed by Jaime Willems
Production by Whitney Schaefer

Design element: Shutterstock: Alexzel, Betelejze,
cuppuccino, wormig

978 1 3982 5321 6

British Library Cataloguing in Publication Data
A full catalogue record for this book is available from
the British Library.

Printed and bound in India.

CONTENTS

MEET JC

Hi! My name is Jalen Corey Pierce, but everyone calls me JC. I am seven years old.

I live with Mum, Dad and my baby sister, Maya. Nana and Pop-Pop live in our block of flats too. So do my two best friends, Amir and Vicky.

My family and I used to live in a small town. Now I live in a big city with tall buildings and lots of people. Come along with me on all my new adventures!

Chapter 1

STUCK INSIDE

JC and his friends had been stuck inside all morning. They wanted to go to the park, but it was raining.

"What else can we do for fun?" JC asked.

"We could play a board game," Amir suggested.

"I'm bored of board games," JC said.

"Me too," Vicky agreed.

They tried to find something else to do. They did some colouring in. They played hide-and-seek.

Finally, the rain stopped.

"Can we go to the park now?"

JC asked Dad.

"Sorry," Dad said. "I need to finish this painting. I have an exhibition soon."

JC was disappointed. They needed a grown-up to go to the park.

A few minutes later, the front door opened. Mum walked into the flat.

"What's with the sad faces?" she asked.

"We're bored! Can we go to the park?" JC begged.

"Let me change out of my scrubs," Mum said. "Then we can go."

"Yay!" JC and his friends cheered.

Chapter 2

A NEW NEIGHBOUR

Mum, JC, Amir and Vicky got the lift to the lobby. When they got off, there were boxes piled everywhere.

"Looks like someone's moving in," Mum said.

"Maybe someone our age is moving in," JC said.

"We can always have more friends!" Amir added.

Just then, a woman walked through the door. Her arms were filled with more boxes.

"Is anyone helping her?"
JC asked.

"I'm not sure," Mum said.
"I'll find out what's going on."

Mum went to talk to the woman. After a minute, they came back together.

"Everyone, meet Mrs Jones,"
Mum said. "She's moving into
a flat on the fifth floor."

"All by yourself?" JC said.
"That's a lot of boxes!"

"My movers had another job
to do today," Mrs Jones explained.
"They'll be back later."

Mum smiled. "I told her we'd help until they return."

JC frowned. "What about the park?" he asked.

"The park will still be there afterwards," Mum said.

Chapter 3

TIME TO HELP

"If we all help, we'll get finished faster," Vicky said.

"I'll get the heavier boxes," Mum said. "You three get the lighter ones."

JC and his friends got to work.

They carried the boxes to the lift.

Mrs Jones then took them to her

flat.

"Moving day is lots of work,"

Amir said.

"Would anyone like some water?" Mrs Jones asked.

"Yes, please!" JC said.

Everyone went upstairs to have a break.

"Where were you all going earlier?" Mrs Jones asked.

"To the park. We've been inside all day," JC answered.

"Somewhere in the removal van is a box of toys," Mrs Jones said. "They're for my grandchildren when they visit. You can take them to the park."

"Really?" JC said.

Mrs Jones smiled. "It'll be your reward!"

JC perked up. Helping Mrs Jones would make going to the park even better!

Chapter 4

BOX OF FUN

Everyone went downstairs to get more boxes. JC spotted the word *TOYS* written on one.

"I've found it!" he exclaimed.

"Wonderful," Mrs Jones replied. "It's the least I can do after your help today."

JC opened the box. Inside

he saw a baseball, a football, a

yo-yo and a Frisbee.

Amir reached into the box of toys. He pulled out a pair of binoculars.

"What are these for?" Amir asked.

"They're for seeing things far away," Mrs Jones said.

"Maybe we could use them to bird-watch at the park," Mum suggested.

"That sounds fun!" Vicky agreed.

Mrs Jones peeked out of the front door.

"Looks like my movers are back," she said. "You should go to the park now."

"Thank you for letting us borrow the toys," JC replied.

Mrs Jones smiled. "And thank *you* for being my moving day helpers."

GLOSSARY

binoculars tool that makes far-away objects look closer

bored no longer interested in something or fed up because you have nothing to do

exhibition display that shows something to the public

lobby hall or entrance area just inside a building

reward something you get for doing something well

scrubs loose, lightweight uniform worn by workers in clinics and hospitals

yo-yo thick, divided disk that is made to fall and rise to the hand by unwinding and rewinding on a string

MOVING DAY REWARD

Mrs Jones let JC and his friends borrow a box of toys to take to the park. What else do you think might have been inside? Use your imagination, and draw a picture of all the toys in the box. Then draw some of the birds JC and his friends might have seen at the park using the binoculars.

LET'S TALK

1. What do you think JC, Amir and Vicky
    did while they were stuck playing inside?
    What board games do you think they
    played? Who do you think won the most
    games?

2. JC and his friends had to wait for a
    grown-up to go to the park. Have you
    ever had to wait to do something fun?
    How did you pass the time?

3. Imagine you are moving or helping
    someone else move home. What is one
    thing you would like about moving? What
    is one thing you might not like? Talk about
    your choices and explain why.

LET'S WRITE

1. The box of toys JC found had a baseball, a football, a yo-yo, a Frisbee and a pair of binoculars. What other toys would you have wanted to find? Make a list.

2. Have you ever written a thank-you note? Imagine you are JC, Amir or Vicky. Try writing a thank-you note to Mrs Jones thanking her for lending you the box of toys.

3. Lots of people move to new houses, flats, cities and towns. Imagine you or a friend are moving away. Practise writing a letter to keep in touch.

Dorothy H Price loves writing stories for young readers. Her first picture book, *Nana's Favorite Things*, is proof of that. Dorothy was a 2019 winner of the We Need Diverse Books Mentorship Program in the United States. She hopes all young readers know they can grow up to write stories too.

Shiane Salabie is a Jamaica-born illustrator based in Philadelphia, USA. When she moved to the United States, she discovered her first true love: the library. Shiane later realized that she wanted to bring stories to life and uses her art to do so.